GRANDDADDY'S

To all of the Coleman, DeGross,
and Johnson men and boys,
then and now.—M. L .DeG.

For information address Hyperion Books for Children, 114 Fifth Avenue, New York, New York 10011-5690.
First Edition   3 5 7 9 10 8 6 4 2
Printed in Singapore
Library of Congress Cataloging-in-Publication Data
DeGross, Monalisa.
Granddaddy's Street Songs / Monalisa DeGross; illustrated by Floyd Cooper—1st ed.   p. cm.
Summary: A grandfather vividly describes to his grandson a typical day from his youth, when he worked as a peddler selling fresh fruits
and vegetables from a horse-drawn wagon throughout the city.
ISBN 0-7868-0160-3 (trade)—ISBN 0-7868-2132-9 (lib.)
[1. Peddlers and peddling—Fiction. 2. Grandfathers—Fiction.] I. Cooper, Floyd, ill. II. Title.
PZ7.D3643Ar 1999   [Fic]—DC20 94-49520

STREET SONGS

MONALISA DeGROSS

ILLUSTRATED BY FLOYD COOPER

JUMP AT THE SUN

HYPERION BOOKS FOR CHILDREN

NEW YORK

"Granddaddy," I say, "tell me a story about long ago, when things weren't like they are today."

"I recall the summer of nineteen hundred and fifty-five," Granddaddy begins with a smile and twirls the ends of his mustache.

"Wait just one minute!" I say, stopping him so I can run and get what we need for a good, long story.

"Easy now," Granddaddy warns as I pull the blue leather photo album from the shelf and bring it to him. I slide the big book on his lap and watch as Granddaddy wipes the cover with his sleeve. I open the cover slowly, this book is so, so old.

"You can begin right here," I say and point to a picture glued on soft black paper.

"Arabbin'? You sure you want to hear about arabbin'?" Granddaddy asks, as if he thinks I've made a mistake.

"Sure do."

"Well, let me see now, where should I start?" He pretends to glance over the pictures before he begins with words that I know by heart.

"Hiii, yup! Hi, yup. Git-di-yup!" Granddaddy click-clucks his tongue to make just the right sounds. The slow toe-heel prance of Granddaddy's horse begins.

"Git it up, Daybreak, it's time to meet the mornin'!" he says. He flips his fingers and in my mind I see the reins gently slap Daybreak's broad mahogany rump.

Granddaddy makes his voice moan and groan until I can hear the wagon creak and crack, slip-slide backward just a bit, and then follow Daybreak down Central Avenue.

"Where y'all going?" I ask.

"We're on our way to the market!" Granddaddy says. "Got to load up at Camden Market."

"There's Mike Coleman standing out in front of his bicycle shop," Granddaddy points out as we head down Baltimore Street. "And right next door is Henry's Harness Shop."

"You gonna stop and say hello?" I want to know.

"Naw, not today," he says. "We got to get to the market."

As I reach over to turn the page Granddaddy says, "Whoa, slow down, Roddy. We don't want to move *too* fast." He pats my hand.

I lean toward the fuzzy black-and-white pictures. "Gee, I'll bet some of these pictures are even older than you are," I say.

"I know the buildings are," Granddaddy says with a laugh.

At the market there are rows and rows of wooden stalls. Each stall is filled with a different type of fruit or vegetable. In some pictures I see fat, funny fish resting on glassy chips of ice. I wave at the men standing beside the stalls. I like the flat straw hats on their heads and the long, shiny aprons that cover their overalls.

"Granddaddy, there are so many kinds of fruits and vegetables. How did you choose?"

"It was easy. I was careful to select only the crispest, freshest, and ripest produce for my wagon," he says proudly.

"Who is that?" I ask pointing to the next picture.

"That's Peeler!" Granddaddy says, looking pleased.

"He sure is wearing some funny-looking pants," I say, giggling.

"Roddy, that's Peeler's gimmick," he explains. "All arabbers had to have something that made them different."

"And did his gimmick work?" I ask.

"Sure did. Peeler had the second-best gimmick on the east side."

"Who had the best?" I ask with a sly smile. Granddaddy winks and moves on.

"Now look here," he says. "There's my wagon all packed and ready to go. There's a water bucket for Daybreak, and plenty of oats for him to eat. My lunch is packed in that hamper, along with my thermos filled with iced coffee. I had plenty of extra baskets—we didn't use paper bags as much as they do nowadays. And right there are my scales. I always carried two sets, and both of them were perfectly balanced."

"Now is it time to get started?" I ask, trying to rush to the next part.

"No, not yet, I got one more thing to add," he says.

"Your gimmick?" I ask, as if I don't know.

"Yes, my big fancy umbrella. It protected my produce from the hot sun. Roddy, there wasn't another umbrella like mine on the entire east side," he says, puffing up his chest.

"Or anywhere else," I add.

I look closely at the next picture, my nose nearly touching it. "That looks like me!"

"Shucks, Roddy, now you know that's not you," Granddaddy says, laughing. "You wasn't even a whisper in nineteen hundred and fifty-five. That's your daddy; he worked with me that summer. He wasn't a bit older than you are now."

"Granddaddy, he looks just like you, and I look just like him. Who do *we* all look like?"

He flips to the front of the album. And there on the first page is Great-granddaddy Slim.

"I guess all the Johnson men look alike," I say proudly, and we nod.

"Granddaddy, I wish the world was in color when you were arabbin'."

"Don't you worry, Roddy. I'm gonna describe things so well, you're gonna feel just like you were there."

"I'm ready," I say. When Granddaddy takes me on his arabbin' ride, I don't know whether to look at the pictures or him. I always try hard to do both.

Granddaddy cups his hands around his mouth and sings out:

Wa-a-a-ter-melons, I got wa-a-a-ter-melons.
Come git my wa-a-a-ter-melons.
Sweet, juicy, juicy, red to the rind.
Red, juicy, red, juicy wa-a-a-ter-melons.
Come git my wa-a-a-ter-melons.
Cantaloupe! Cantaloupe!
Honeydew! Honeydew!
Melons, melons, and melons.
I got melons, melons, and melons.

I love hearing Granddaddy's calls—they sound like songs. I begin to pat my feet to the rhythm of his voice, as he sings out loud and clear:

> *If you like what you hear*
> *Then you'll love what you see.*
> *Peaches, peaches, yes, sirree.*
> *Round, fuzzy, firm, and ripe!*
> *I'll betcha need a bib with every bite.*

All morning Granddaddy and Daybreak clip up cobblestoned streets and clop down narrow brick alleys, selling to old customers and meeting new ones as they travel along. I see babies waving, kids bouncing balls, and people laughing and talking, trying to decide just what to buy. And Granddaddy's calls help them make up their minds:

> *Ce-le-ry, long, green, and fine.*
> *If you give me a quarter, I'll give back a dime.*
> *Listen to me sing. Listen to me holler.*
> *Listen while I tell what I got for a dollar.*
> *Yellow onions—I got 'em.*
> *Summer squash—I got 'em.*
> *Got peppers, green and red.*
> *Got them hotter than you ever had.*
> *Open your doors, come out and see.*
> *Don't buy from others, just buy from me.*

When Granddaddy stops to take a deep breath, I ask,
"Can I join you?"

"Roddy, you don't need to ask, just jump right in,"
he says, giving me a hug.

Cherries, cherries—sweet, dark cherries.
And straw-berries, straw-berries, red strawberries.
I said sweet, dark cherries and red strawberries.
Lettuce! Lettuce! Lettuce!
Let us sell you lettuce an-n-nd
Red ripe tomatoes,
Fat brown potatoes,
Sweet silver corn.
Cherries, berries, lettuce, tomatoes, potatoes, and corn.
Cherries, berries, lettuce, tomatoes, potatoes, and corn.

On and on Granddaddy and I sing and call, looking at pictures of people and places from a time long ago, before I was born. And when we see the empty wagon and there is nothing more to buy or sell, we know it's time for our last call:

> We've been travelin', travelin', travelin' far,
> And nothing we've sold you comes from a jar.
> Our wagon is empty, there's nothing to sell.
> So Daybreak and I must bid you farewell!

"Whew! That was fun," I say as we settle back on the sofa.

"Roddy," Granddaddy says, "we've been arabbin' so much, I'm just plain worn out."

I point to the last picture. "Where y'all going?" I ask.

"Shucks, I'm taking Daybreak home, he's had a long, hard day."

Granddaddy's voice is soft with memories and so is mine when I say, "So have I."

HISTORICAL NOTE

Many cities and towns in America have a tradition of street vendors selling goods and wares from horse-drawn wagons. Baltimore, Maryland, shares that tradition with one unique twist—the name by which its street vendors were known: arabbers. The origin of the name has been debated, with most scholars tracing its use to slang from nineteenth-century London, describing someone without a fixed home or place. In Baltimore, however, the terms "ay-rab" and "arabber" conjure vivid images of African-American men, selling primarily fruits, vegetables, and seafood throughout the many communities of the city. These men developed individual calls as well as special names and decorations for their horses, which were an important part of the team. They worked hard and rose early to ensure the freshness of what they were selling and to catch the attention of buyers before their fellow vendors could. Children were especially drawn to arabbers, attracted by the music and color they brought to the Baltimore neighborhoods.

Deborah Taylor
Enoch Pratt Free Library
Baltimore, Maryland